OUR LADY OF PERPETUAL HELP

P9-AOW-993
Woodwind instruments

714 REI

Woodwind Instruments

Music Makers

THE CHILD'S WORLD®, INC.

Woodwind Instruments

Elizabeth Reid

THE CHILD'S WORLD®, INC.

On the cover: Three of these girls are playing woodwind instruments.

Published in the United States of America by The Child's World®, Inc.
PO Box 326
Chanhassen, MN 55317-0326
800-599-READ
www.childsworld.com

Product Manager Mary Berendes
Editor Katherine Stevenson, Ph.D.

Copyright © 2003 by The Child's World®, Inc.
All rights reserved. No part of this book may be
reproduced or utilized in any form or by any means
without written permission from the publisher.

Library of Congress Cataloging-in-Publication Data
Reid, Elizabeth, 1968–
Woodwind instruments / by Elizabeth Reid.
     p. cm.
Includes index.
ISBN 1-56766-988-3 (lib. bdg. : alk. paper)
1. Woodwind instruments—Juvenile literature.
[1. Woodwind instruments.]   I. Title.
ML931 .R45 2002
788.2'19—dc21
                              2001006025

Photo Credits
© Arvind Garg/CORBIS: 13
© Charles & Josette Lenars/CORBIS: 9
© CORBIS: 23 (bass flute, bassoon, clarinet, flute, oboe, recorder)
© Corbis Stock Market/John Henley: cover, 2
© Dave G. Houser/CORBIS: 16
© Michael and Patricia Fogden/CORBIS: 6
© PhotoDisc: 23 (piccolo, saxophone, slide whistle)
© Steve Cole/PhotoDisc/PictureQuest: 19
© Wolfgang Kaehler/CORBIS: 10
© www.corbis.com/Ric Ergenbright: 20
© www.corbis.com/Ted Streshinsky: 15

Table of Contents

Woodwind Instruments

Musical instruments are wonderful things. They can make all sorts of sounds, from the deep BOOM-BOOM of thunder to the mysterious WHO-WHOOO of an owl. Instruments can make music sound happy or sad. Sometimes instruments can even sound as if they are talking to each other!

← This man is charming a snake with a wooden flute in Pakistan.

Woodwind instruments make sounds when you blow air through them. They can make lots of different sounds. Saxophones, clarinets, flutes, and recorders are examples of woodwind instruments.

This Indonesian man is playing a *silingut*, → or nose flute. He plays the flute by blowing air through his nose instead of his mouth.

What Are Woodwinds Made Of?

Woodwind instruments have been around for thousands of years. Some of the earliest flutes and recorders were made of hollowed-out animal bones! Most early woodwinds, however, were made of wood. In fact, that is why they are called "woodwinds." Today some woodwind instruments are still made of wood. More of them, however, are now made of metal, hard rubber, or plastic.

← These men from the Solomon Islands are playing homemade pan flutes.

What Do Woodwinds Look Like?

No matter what they are made of, most woodwind instruments have the same basic shape and parts. One important part is the **mouthpiece**. You blow into the mouthpiece to make a sound. In flutes, the mouthpiece is just a hole that you blow air across. Some other woodwinds have other kinds of mouthpieces.

This girl in India is playing a flute called a *bansuri*. ➔

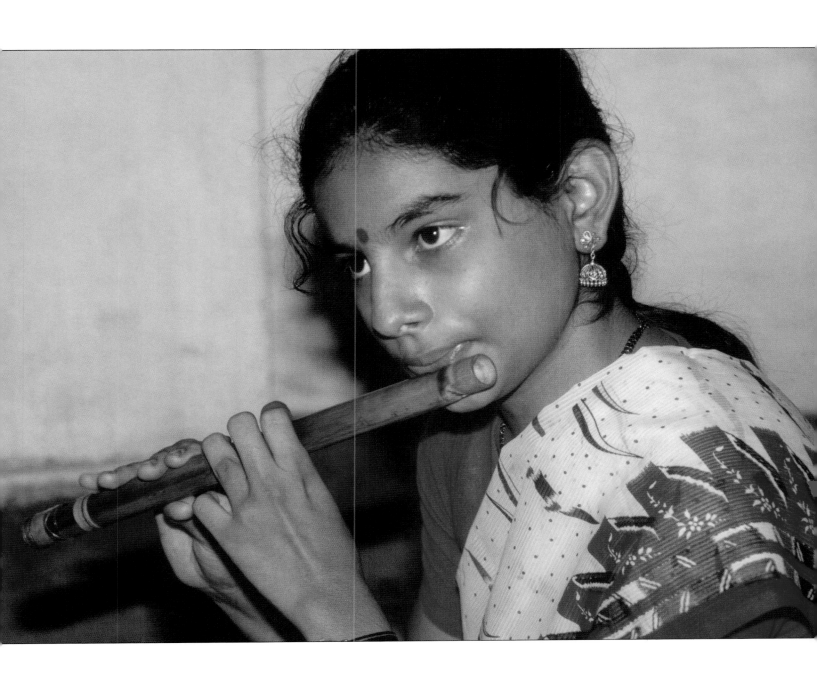

The biggest part of a woodwind instrument is its body. The body is basically a hollow tube. The tube has many holes. Usually the holes are covered by small metal pieces called **keys**. Smaller woodwinds, such as the tiny 12-inch piccolo, have straight bodies. Others, such as the giant 16-foot contrabassoon, have curved bodies.

There are many keys on the soprano ➔
saxophone this man is playing.

Different Kinds of Woodwinds

Woodwind instruments can be divided into two groups. Some woodwinds make sounds when you blow air straight into the instrument or across the mouthpiece hole. Flutes and recorders belong to this group. Other woodwinds make sound when you blow air around a thin piece of wood called a **reed**. Some woodwinds, such as saxophones and clarinets, have one reed. Others, such as bassoons and oboes, have two reeds connected to a thin tube.

← This man is playing a beautifully carved flute in Bali.

How Do Woodwinds Make Sounds?

Woodwind instruments make sound when the air inside them moves quickly back and forth, or **vibrates**. In flutes, the air starts vibrating when it hits the sharp edge of the mouthpiece hole. In saxophones and other reed instruments, the reed vibrates when you blow air around it. The vibrating reed causes the air in the instrument's body to vibrate.

Here you can see the reed on the mouthpiece of this clarinet. →

How Do You Play Woodwind Instruments?

Different kinds of woodwinds are held different ways when you play them. To play a flute or a piccolo, you hold it sideways. To play most other woodwind instruments, you hold them straight in front of you.

When you hold the instrument, your fingers cover the holes or keys on its body. Woodwinds can have only a few holes or more than 20. Covering different holes or leaving them open makes the air in the tube travel different distances. The shorter the distance, the higher the sound the instrument makes.

← This man is using his fingers to cover many of the holes on a wooden flute.

What Do Woodwind Instruments Sound Like?

Woodwind instruments are popular because they can produce many different sounds. They can make notes that sound high, or have a high **pitch**. They can make notes that have a low pitch. They can also produce many different types of sound, or **tones**. The sounds of woodwinds can be loud or soft, happy or sad, sweet or forceful.

Because of their many uses, woodwinds have always been a favorite choice of musicians. Now that you know more about them, maybe you'll want to play a woodwind, too!

Other Woodwind Instruments

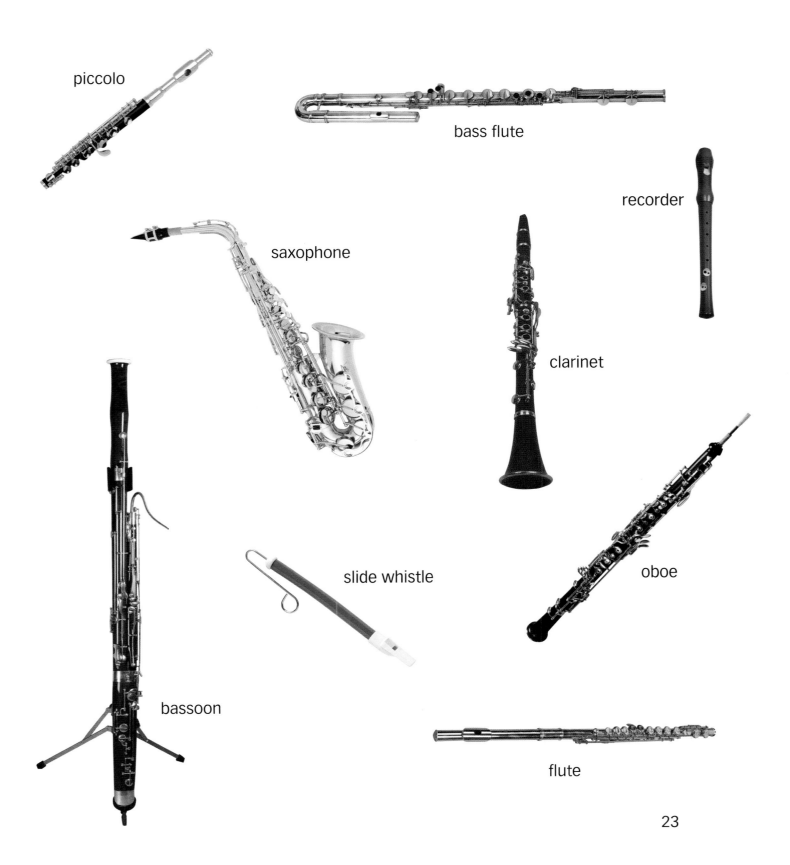

piccolo

bass flute

recorder

saxophone

clarinet

bassoon

slide whistle

oboe

flute

Glossary

keys (KEEZ)
On a woodwind instrument, the keys are small metal flaps that open or close over holes in the body. Opening or closing the holes changes the notes the instrument produces.

mouthpiece (MOUTH-peece)
The mouthpiece is the part of an instrument where you hold your mouth to play. Different kinds of wind instruments have different kinds of mouthpieces.

pitch (PITCH)
In music, pitch is how high or low a sound is. Woodwind instruments can make sounds of many different pitches.

reed (REED)
On a woodwind instrument, a reed is a thin piece of wood or plastic that vibrates when you blow air over it. The vibrating reed produces sound.

tones (TOHNZ)
In music, tone is a note's quality, or the way it sounds. Woodwinds can produce many different tones.

vibrates (VY-brayts)
When something vibrates, it moves back and forth very quickly. In a woodwind instrument, vibrating air produces sound.

Index

7140